THE TALE

OF

Mrs. TITTLEMOUSE

THE TALE OF
Mrs. TITTLEMOUSE

By

BEATRIX POTTER

Author of
"The Tale of Peter Rabbit" etc.

BLOOMSBURY BOOKS
in association with
FREDERICK WARNE

BLOOMSBURY BOOKS IN ASSOCIATION WITH FREDERICK WARNE

Published by the Penguin Group
Penguin Books Ltd, 27 Wrights Lane, London W8 5TZ, England
Penguin Books USA Inc., 375 Hudson Street, New York, N.Y. 10014, USA
Penguin Books Australia Ltd, Ringwood, Victoria, Australia
Penguin Books Canada Ltd, 10 Alcorn Avenue, Toronto, Ontario, Canada M4V 3B2
Penguin Books (N.Z.) Ltd, 182-190 Wairau Road, Auckland 10, New Zealand

Penguin Books Ltd, Registered Offices: Harmondsworth, Middlesex, England

Bloomsbury Books, an imprint of The Godfrey Cave Group,
42 Bloomsbury Street, London WC1B 3QJ

First published by Frederick Warne & Co. 1910
Published with new reproductions 1987
This edition first published 1993

ISBN 1 85471 375 2

Printed and bound in Great Britain by
William Clowes Limited, Beccles and London

NELLIE'S
LITTLE BOOK

8

ONCE upon a time there was a wood-mouse, and her name was Mrs. Tittle-mouse.

She lived in a bank under a hedge.

S UCH a funny house !
There were yards and
yards of sandy passages,
leading to storerooms and
nut-cellars and seed-cellars,
all amongst the roots of the
hedge.

11

12

THERE was a kitchen, a parlour, a pantry, and a larder.

Also, there was Mrs. Tittle-mouse's bedroom, where she slept in a little box bed !

MRS. TITTLEMOUSE was a most terribly tidy particular little mouse, always sweeping and dusting the soft sandy floors.

Sometimes a beetle lost its way in the passages.

" Shuh ! shuh ! little dirty feet ! " said Mrs. Tittlemouse, clattering her dust-pan.

15

16

AND one day a little old woman ran up and down in a red spotty cloak.

"Your house is on fire, Mother Ladybird! Fly away home to your children!"

ANOTHER day, a big fat spider came in to shelter from the rain.

" Beg pardon, is this not Miss Muffet's ? "

" Go away, you bold bad spider ! Leaving ends of cobweb all over my nice clean house ! "

SHE bundled the spider out at a window.

He let himself down the hedge with a long thin bit of string.

Mrs. TITTLEMOUSE went on her way to a distant storeroom, to fetch cherry-stones and thistle-down seed for dinner.

All along the passage she sniffed, and looked at the floor.

" I smell a smell of honey ; is it the cowslips outside, in the hedge ? I am sure I can see the marks of little dirty feet."

23

SUDDENLY round a corner, she met Babbitty Bumble —" Zizz, Bizz, Bizzz ! " said the bumble bee.

Mrs. Tittlemouse looked at her severely. She wished that she had a broom.

"Good-day, Babbitty Bumble; I should be glad to buy some beeswax. But what are you doing down here ? Why do you always come in at a window, and say Zizz, Bizz,. Bizzz ? " Mrs. Tittlemouse began to get cross.

"ZIZZ, Wizz, Wizzz !" replied Babbitty Bumble in a peevish squeak. She sidled down a passage, and disappeared into a storeroom which had been used for acorns.

Mrs. Tittlemouse had eaten the acorns before Christmas ; the storeroom ought to have been empty.

But it was full of untidy dry moss.

27

MRS. TITTLEMOUSE began to pull out the moss. Three or four other bees put their heads out, and buzzed fiercely.

"I am not in the habit of letting lodgings; this is an intrusion!" said Mrs. Tittlemouse. "I will have them turned out—" "Buzz! Buzz! Buzzz!"—"I wonder who would help me?" "Bizz, Wizz, Wizzz!"

—"I will not have Mr. Jackson; he never wipes his feet."

MRS. TITTLEMOUSE decided to leave the bees till after dinner.

When she got back to the parlour, she heard some one coughing in a fat voice ; and there sat Mr. Jackson himself !

He was sitting all over a small rocking-chair, twiddling his thumbs and smiling, with his feet on the fender.

He lived in a drain below the hedge, in a very dirty wet ditch.

32

"HOW do you do, Mr. Jackson? Deary me, you have got very wet!"

"Thank you, thank you, thank you, Mrs. Tittlemouse! I'll sit awhile and dry myself," said Mr. Jackson.

He sat and smiled, and the water dripped off his coat tails. Mrs. Tittlemouse went round with a mop.

HE sat such a while that he had to be asked if he would take some dinner?

First she offered him cherry-stones. "Thank you, thank you, Mrs. Tittlemouse! No teeth, no teeth, no teeth!" said Mr. Jackson.

He opened his mouth most unnecessarily wide; he certainly had not a tooth in his head.

35

THEN she offered him thistle - down seed — " Tiddly, widdly, widdly ! Pouff, pouff, puff ! " said Mr. Jackson. He blew the thistle-down all over the room.

" Thank you, thank you, thank you, Mrs. Tittlemouse ! Now what I really—*really* should like—would be a little dish of honey ! "

"I AM afraid I have not got any, Mr. Jackson" said Mrs. Tittlemouse.

"Tiddly, widdly, widdly, Mrs. Tittlemouse!" said the smiling Mr. Jackson, "I can *smell* it; that is why I came to call."

Mr. Jackson rose ponderously from the table, and began to look into the cupboards.

Mrs. Tittlemouse followed him with a dish-cloth, to wipe his large wet footmarks off the parlour floor.

38

WHEN he had convinced himself that there was no honey in the cupboards, he began to walk down the passage.

"Indeed, indeed, you will stick fast, Mr. Jackson!"

"Tiddly, widdly, widdly, Mrs. Tittlemouse!"

FIRST he squeezed into the pantry.

" Tiddly, widdly, widdly ? no honey ? no honey, Mrs. Tittlemouse ? "

There were three creepy-crawly people hiding in the plate-rack. Two of them got away ; but the littlest one he caught.

43

THEN he squeezed into the larder. Miss Butterfly was tasting the sugar; but she flew away out of the window.

"Tiddly, widdly, widdly, Mrs. Tittlemouse; you seem to have plenty of visitors!"

"And without any invitation!" said Mrs. Thomasina Tittlemouse.

THEY went along the sandy passage—" Tiddly widdly—" " Buzz ! Wizz ! Wizz ! "

He met Babbitty round a corner, and snapped her up, and put her down again.

" I do not like bumble bees. They are all over bristles," said Mr. Jackson, wiping his mouth with his coat-sleeve.

" Get out, you nasty old toad ! " shrieked Babbitty Bumble.

" I shall go distracted ! " scolded Mrs. Tittlemouse.

48

SHE shut herself up in the nut-cellar while Mr. Jackson pulled out the bees-nest. He seemed to have no objection to stings.

When Mrs. Tittlemouse ventured to come out—everybody had gone away.

But the untidiness was something dreadful—" Never did I see such a mess—smears of honey ; and moss, and thistledown—and marks of big and little dirty feet—all over my nice clean house ! "

SHE gathered up the moss and the remains of the beeswax.

Then she went out and fetched some twigs, to partly close up the front door.

" I will make it too small for Mr. Jackson ! "

SHE fetched soft soap, and flannel, and a new scrubbing brush from the storeroom. But she was too tired to do any more. First she fell asleep in her chair, and then she went to bed.

"Will it ever be tidy again?" said poor Mrs. Tittlemouse.

NEXT morning she got up very early and began a spring cleaning which lasted a fortnight.

She swept, and scrubbed, and dusted ; and she rubbed up the furniture with beeswax, and polished her little tin spoons.

WHEN it was all beauti-
fully neat and clean,
she gave a party to five other
little mice, without Mr.
Jackson.

He smelt the party and
came up the bank, but he
could not squeeze in at the
door.

57

So they handed him out acorn-cupfuls of honey-dew through the window, and he was not at all offended.

He sat outside in the sun, and said—" Tiddly, widdly, widdly! Your very good health, Mrs. Tittlemouse!"

THE END